Gwan
Anthology

VOLUME TWO

Copyright © 2020 Forward Comix. All rights reserved.

No part of this book may be reproduced or transmitted, either in printed or electronic form. No portions of this book may be incorporated or bundled with any other publication, either printed or electronic, without the express written permission of the copyright owner.

The Gwan Anthology, Volume Two is made possible by the generous contributions of independent writers, artists, and comic creators. Each contributor (team) retains and reserves all rights pertaining to his, her, or its respective work.

Forward Comix
Brooklyn, New York
www.forwardcomix.com

ISBN: 978-1-7344969-0-1

Library of Congress Control Number: 2020931672

Gwan
Anthology

Could a common greeting, familiar to a tiny Caribbean region, start a conversation that embraces the whole world?

- Artists/Writers who are currently living in this country
  Australia, Canada, Georgia, Germany, Indonesia, Italy, Spain, Singapore, Trinidad
- Artists / Writers who are immigrants from this country
- Artists / Writers who have lived in this country for more than one year
  Argentina, England, France, Israel, Jamaica, the Philippines
- Artists / Writers who have based their stories on experiences of loved ones from this country
- Artists / Writers who have close family from this country
  Japan, Russia, South Africa, St. Kitts, Vietnam
- Artists/Writers who are expats from this country and other artists / writers who are currently living in this country
  China, United States
- Entries meant to highlight refugee experiences in these areas
  Mexico, Saudi Arabia, Yemen
- Artists / Writers who are descendants of immigrants from this country
  Russia

FORWARD COMIX

JEROME WALFORD
Managing Editor

Editor's Letter: Being Fruitful

There is a common spiritual practice observed by monks in remote locations and also by some well-to-do. The practice is to live for a time or a lifetime under a vow of poverty. It begs the question, what is so desirable about being poor? There is the classic argument – overabundance is highly problematic. It often blinds us to things of true worth so that we tend to forget what it's like to be in want, and we lose the ability to be empathetic to those who struggle economically. All of that may be enough for one to pause and reconsider how we treat those who live in poverty not by choice, much less a glorified version of the same.

Having grown up for a portion of my childhood where being poor was so pervasive it was simply "the way it is," I am sure of this: we didn't consider ourselves to be poor. By that I mean it was not a primary part of our identity. We were aware of our poor situation, and we had friends in more impoverished circumstances than our own, yet none of us were poor. Let that seed sit for a minute.

Why do some choose poverty while others have it thrust upon them? Perhaps there is an intangible worth only brought about by desperate circumstances. If we have forgotten, we only need a moment of observation, a second of reflection: most of the richness we experience in life – economically, culturally, or otherwise, is born out of poverty. There are certain depths of character, ingenuity, and persistence, that can only be cultivated by being buried under that kind of pressure. It is rather amazing to take in decay, darkness, brokenness, and dirt, yet give birth to beauty, culture, life, food, and occasionally, shiny objects.

Who would've ever thought that a little boy, inspired by a rat in his wall, would eventually found a company which now dominates how we entertain ourselves? Who would have guessed that the poor inner cities of America would soon spawn entirely new forms of visual, musical, and lyrical art that many would pay millions to experience and copy?

Am I saying that we should toss all our possessions? Not necessarily, though I hope we will be moved towards generosity. At the very least, I do think we should be wary of calling another's poverty and location names that show dishonor to the human struggle. We should not despise the "least among us", particularly the alien, immigrant, and refugee. The struggle to escape rot and decay is often what makes us the most fruitful.

Enjoy volume two of the Gwan Anthology. It was a rewarding experience creating it.

SANKOFARRATION

I have been thinking a lot about sowing the right seeds for the future, and also how history plays a part in people from various spaces needing to hold on to their culture.

JOHN JENNINGS
United States
Instagram @johnjenningsart

let the LITTLE CHILDREN

"LET THE LITTLE CHILDREN COME TO ME,

...AND DO NOT HINDER THEM,

FOR THE KINGDOM OF GOD....

BELONGS TO SUCH AS THESE"

MATTHEW 19:14, NEW INTERNATIONAL VERSION

JEROME WALFORD

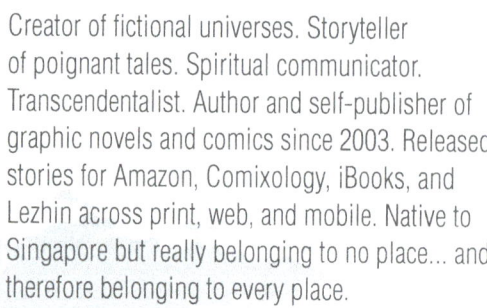

JOHNY TAY
Writer
Singapore

johnytay.net

Creator of fictional universes. Storyteller of poignant tales. Spiritual communicator. Transcendentalist. Author and self-publisher of graphic novels and comics since 2003. Released stories for Amazon, Comixology, iBooks, and Lezhin across print, web, and mobile. Native to Singapore but really belonging to no place... and therefore belonging to every place.

JAMES O'REILLY
Artist
Australia

Instagram @jamesoreillyart
james-oreilly.com

James is an Australian artist based in Asia. He studied animation and has worked for many years as a freelance artist, primarily in video games, with additional experience in comics, book illustration, and various other areas.

James is also involved in the fine arts, creating sculptures and digital paintings. He has exhibited in several cities including London, Amsterdam, and Brisbane.

Art is at the core of James' life, and alongside that is the art of living. To this end he is a dedicated practitioner of meditation, and it has both informed and improved his art and all other aspects of his life. Comics have increasingly become more central to James' work, and he is presently writing and illustrating his own comic.

Now imagine you zoom out into hyperspace. Blinding, racing lights of all possible colors pass you in your tunnel.

With those blinding lights you hear sounds zipping by so rapidly and making such a high-pitched din that they deafen your ears.

Now the pitch of the sounds go lower and lower... until all you hear is a deep, thundering drone. The drone turns solid, enveloping you.

Now that drone becomes vibrations doing their little dances and passing through you.

**MIGUEL GUERRA
SUZY DIAS**
United States / Spain / Europe

Instagram
@miguelguerra1532
@suzydias1

7robots.com

On a typical day, Miguel Guerra gives historical tours of Paris. By night he's hunched over his drawing desk, squinting into the red-eyed hours of the morning, basking in the chaos of creating comics and freelance illustrations.

By day, Suzy Dias is an English teacher in Paris, but after hours she's a devotee at the church of pencraft, where she spends countless hours forging plots and writing comics. With a propensity for crochet, she also creates quirky toys, hats, and anything slightly weird.

Among their notable achievements are publishing short stories in *Heavy Metal* ("Bedbugs" in July 2007, "Insomnia" in January 2010, and "A Lonely Cry in Space" in May 2010) and having *Samurai Elf* picked up by the New York Public Library.

MICHELINE HESS
Writer / Artist
United States

facebook.com/ovenland
Twitter @michMashArts
Instagram @michmasharts

Born and raised in New York City, with family roots in St. Vincent, Micheline Hess started her professional comic book career in the early '90s with Milestone Comics as a colorist. She has several creator-owned works such as the award-winning, fantasy-adventure comic book series *Malice in Ovenland*, the children's book *The Island Cats of Cunga Ree*, and *The Anansi Kids and the All Saints' Day Adventure*. The notion of exploring her own West Indian roots through telling stories that focus on Afro-Caribbean folklore and culture was the driving force behind *The Anansi Kids* comic, and she definitely plans to make more of these stories.

In addition to being an independent comic book creator, Micheline is also an accomplished digital painter, with her work shown nationally at various art shows annually. Her work has also appeared in *The New Yorker* magazine online.

Micheline is most adept at creating characters and stories that provide a safe and fun way to inspire young children, especially girls. Through colorful flights of fun and fancy, she hopes to encourage a stronger sense of self-love, friendship, and a hunger to embrace all things new and different in the world around them.

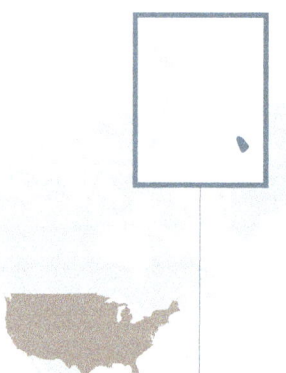

Remember during the tour, when the guide talked about how rowboats loaded down with huge barrels of sugar would be rowed out to sea? Only the Caribs could handle this dangerous job. Their strength and knowledge of the sea was unmatched. They needed that to navigate the treacherous current just offshore.

According to the story on the Boozy Legends website, one row boat had a stash of powerful rum hidden away beneath the seats. It's believed it was to be presented as a "gift" to the captain of the ship.

But a powerful wave slammed into them, damaging the boat.

The men got caught in the fearsome current...

...and they were pulled beneath the churning waves, never to be seen again.

They say that the wreckage is only reachable during a SUPER BLOOD MOON! The tide's especially low during that time, so we might be able to find it more easily.. Otherwise, we won't have another chance for 28 years! If we can find the stash, and reverse engineer the recipe...

WE CAN MAKE MILLIONS!

AYOMIDE OMOBO
Writer
Nigeria / United States

Ayomide Omobo is a freelance writer based in Washington, DC. She is a Nigerian-born Black immigrant woman, writer, law student and fangirl of all things relating to Black women. She enjoys writing characters at the intersection of Blackness, gender, and sexuality, and the politics that surround marginalized identities. In *Osun*, four women – Yemoja, Angela, Alexis, and Jamilah, are all touched irrevocably by police brutality and institutionalized racism. Alexis, following an interaction with the agents of the state, is reborn as Osun, a powerful goddess who wields water as a weapon. Empowered, she makes the decision to go after the people who took everything from her and who criminalize being Black and/or Brown. She, with Jamilah by her side, goes after a group that wields money and power as their weapon of choice – the Company, a group of white supremacists that orchestrate the systematic violence against Black and Brown people. Along the way, Osun is forced to decide what she will and will not do to protect the people she loves.

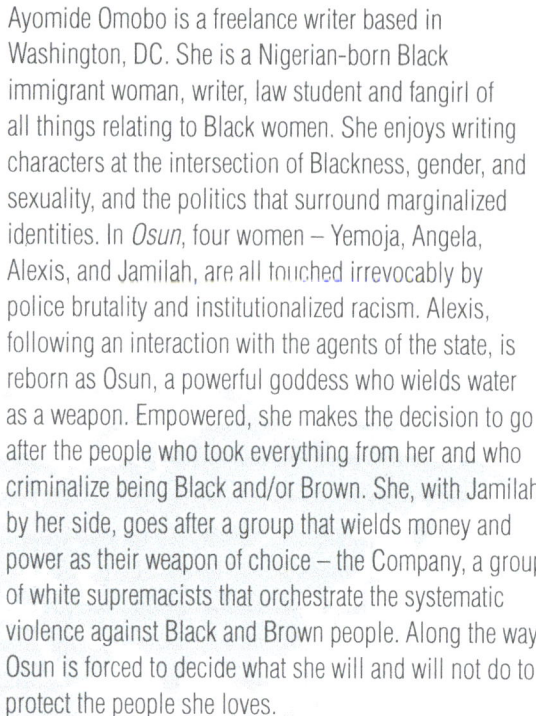

AMARI HARKNESS
Illustrator
United States

Amari Harkness is a freelance illustrator, animator, and 3D artist. She graduated from Savannah College of Art and Design with a BFA. She was a participant artist in the ASIFA-SOUTH Creative Incubator 2018 for the Mike Rowe webseries S.W.E.A.T. Pledge, and worked as an illustrator for the animated opening sequence of a documentary about *Redemptive Cycles' Tall Bike Joust*. On a personal side of things, Amari likes to write fantasy stories and create odd worlds of the strange and the unusual.

KOKAB ZOHOORI-DOSSA
Colorist
Jamaica / United States

Kokab Zohoori-Dossa is a freelance illustrator from Kingston, Jamaica, with a Bachelors Degree in Fine Arts, and the accumulation of a subsequent four years in the professional freelance practice. Her style is a unique amalgamation of her favorite influences, from novels to animation, film, and even music. She also pulls heavily from her own Jamaican heritage, as well as from her Persian and Benin ancestry, all of which are projected in her work through a unique contemporary lens.

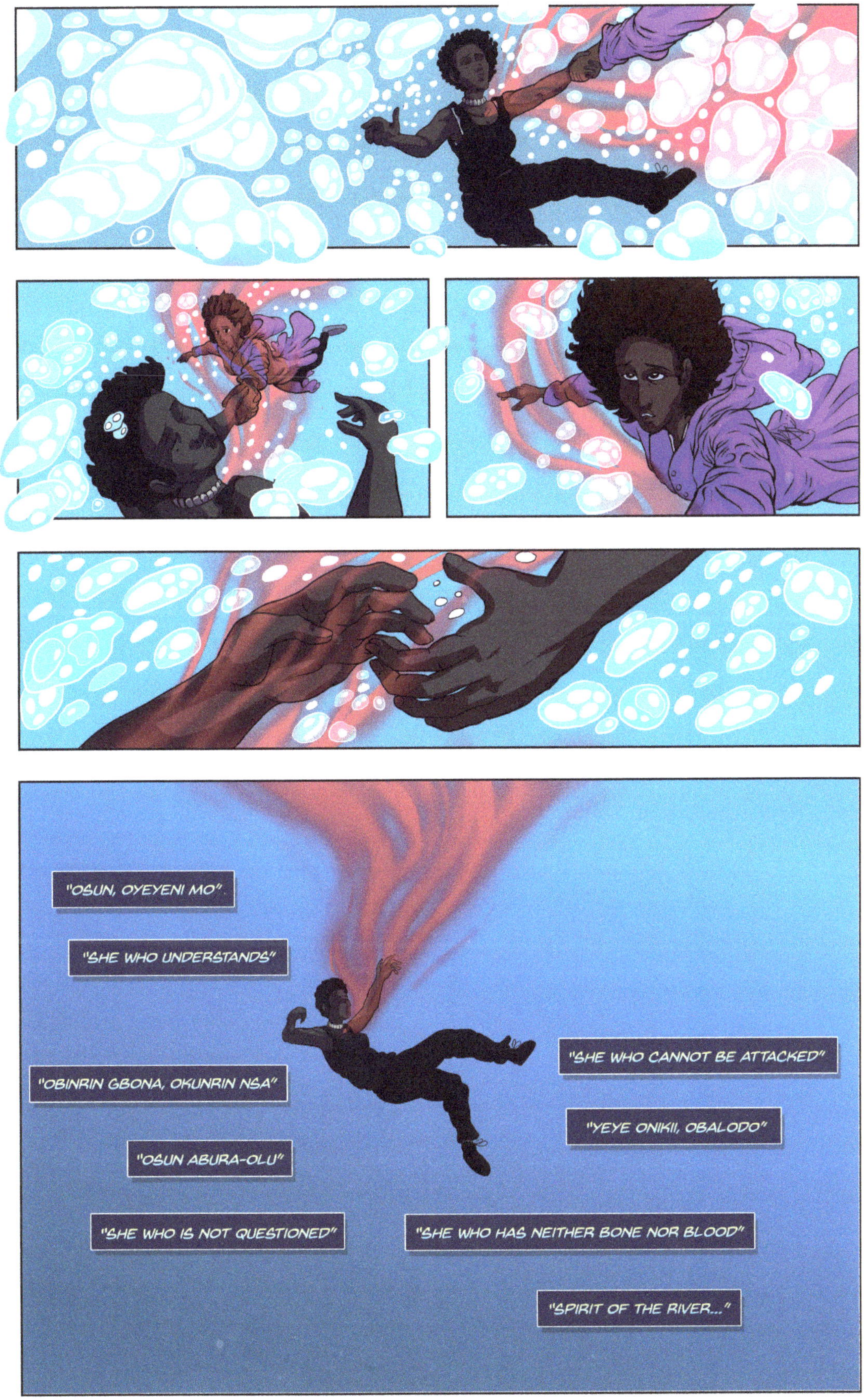

"OSUN, OYEYENI MO".

"SHE WHO UNDERSTANDS"

"OBINRIN GBONA, OKUNRIN NSA"

"OSUN ABURA-OLU"

"SHE WHO IS NOT QUESTIONED"

"SHE WHO CANNOT BE ATTACKED"

"YEYE ONIKII, OBALODO"

"SHE WHO HAS NEITHER BONE NOR BLOOD"

"SPIRIT OF THE RIVER..."

MOTHER DAUGHTER   JEROME WALFORD   INSTAGRAM @FORWARDCOMIX

ORGANIZING IS THE NEW COOL

C.Flux Sing has made Atlanta his home for more than a decade. Sing has a penchant for using vibrant color schemes, which captivatingly tell a true story of the Black experience. Inspired by comic books, graffiti, abstract art, design, urban decay, and surrealism, C.Flux is driven to do something new that pushes the boundaries.

CRAIG CFLUX SINGLETON
United States
Instagram @cfluxsing
cfluxsing.com

SCOOTER DOWN   JEROME WALFORD   INSTAGRAM @FORWARDCOMIX

ESCAPING PANDEMONIUM

BY ABELARD ALEXIS

ABELARD ALEXIS
Writer / Artist
United States

Instagram @abeillustrations
abelardillustrations.com

Abelard is a freelance illustrator from Brooklyn, New York, who finds joy in evoking emotions by way of visual storytelling with his art. He's been drawing since he was seven years old, inspired by the early works of *Dragon Ball Z* and *Naruto*. His inspiration led him to making his own stories and creating his own characters for leisure. Later, Abelard made the decision that illustration would be his dream career and attended FIT (Fashion Institute of Technology) where he graduated with his BFA (Bachelor of Fine Arts) degree. Today, Abelard is expanding his art and career by doing freelance client work, as well as writing and illustrating his own comics. The first issue of his comic, *Alternia*, is currently in production, but artwork of the characters' designs, and finished illustrations of scenes from the story are on his website, and are even sold at conventions.

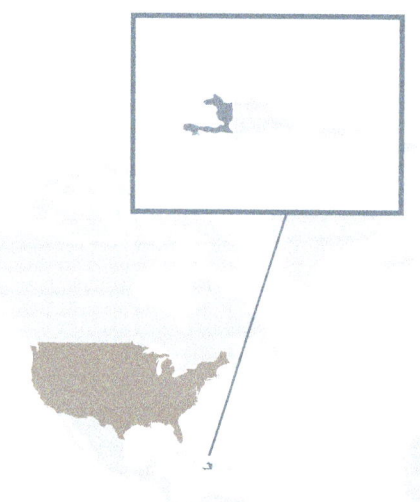

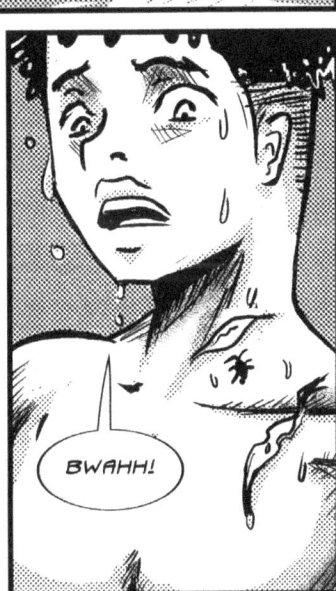

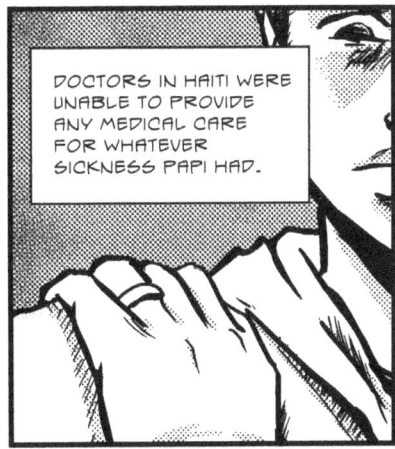

JARRET KATZ
Writer / Artist
United States

jkatzstudio.artstation.com
Instagram @jkatzstudio
Twitter @jkatzstudio

Jarret Katz is a full-time freelance comic book artist based out of Seattle, Washington. After going full time in November 2018, Jarret has worked on a number of comic book titles including *Eden*, issues one through three; Inflection Point Studio title, *Four*; *The Chimera Club*, issue one; Digital Hand Studio title, *The Foreigner*, issues one and two; and a number of short anthology pieces. While mainly a penciler and inker, *Coming to Earth* is a unique story in which Jarret wrote, drew, colored, and lettered the entire story with some crucial help from Jerome.

Jarret is the great-grandson of Russian-Jewish immigrants who came to America in 1917 to escape persecution from the pogroms and the violence of World War I. After immigrating through Ellis Island and having their last names changed, Jarret's grandparents settled in New England to start their lives anew.

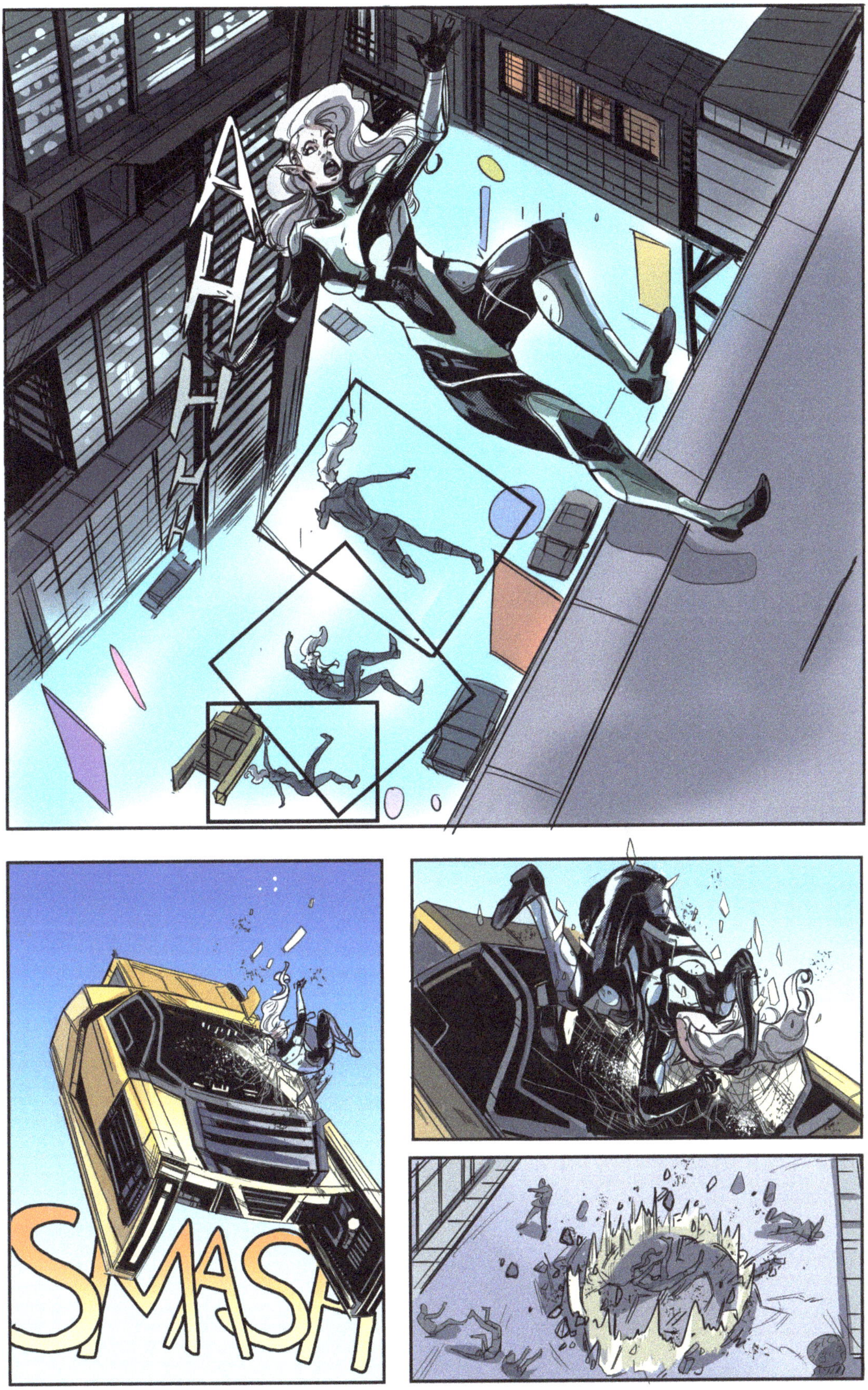

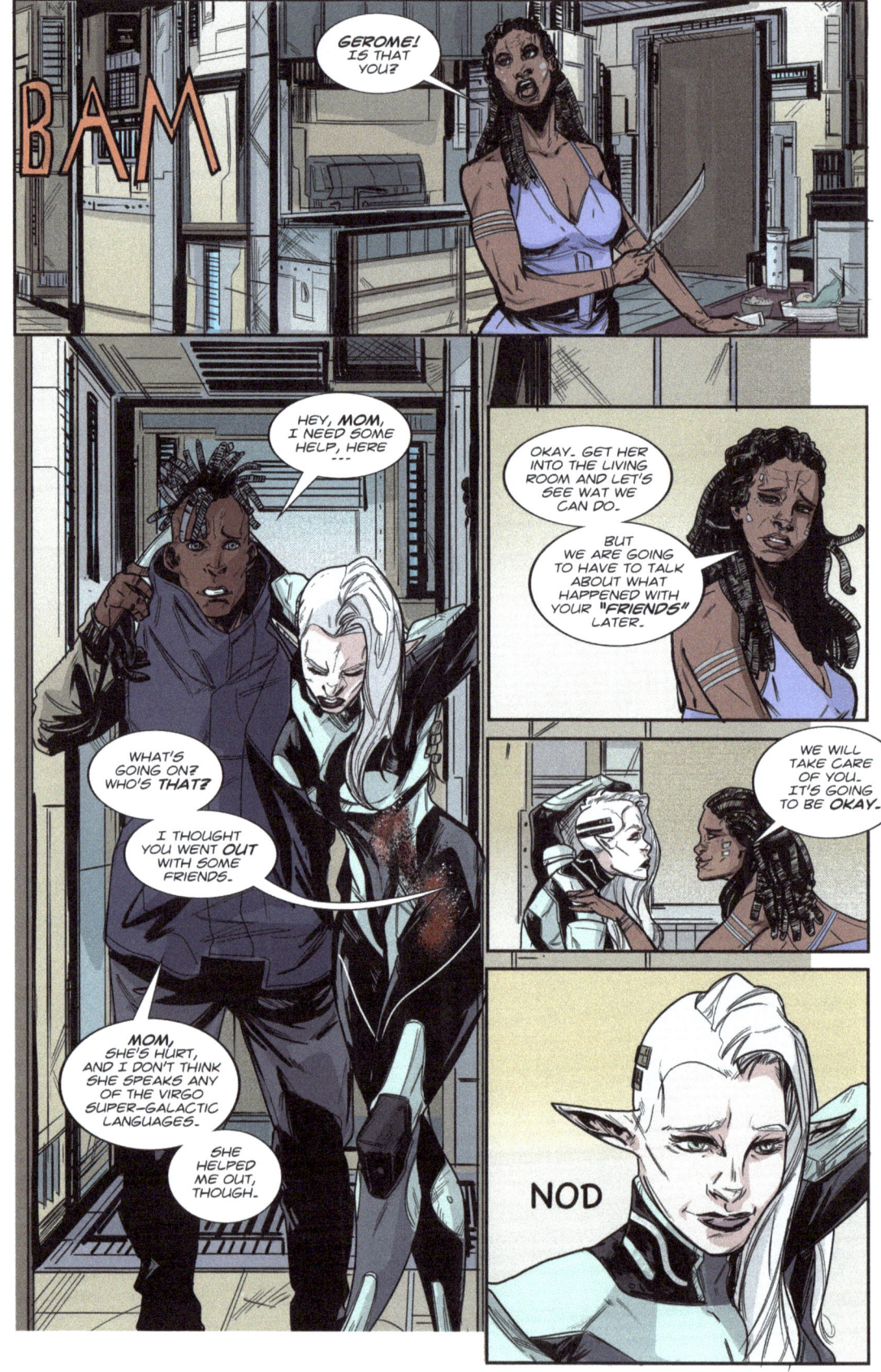

TARA NAVAL
Writer
Spain / Italy / Australia

Instagram @temporiumart
fb.com/temporiumatelier

Tara is a bedroom goblin who enjoys painting, writing, and keeping her hands busy. She is currently obsessed with oil paints and making soap.

Tara (a confusing mix of Filipino and South African heritage), emigrated from her birth country of Spain to Australia. After a few years, she moved again and lived in various countries in Europe including Italy, the Netherlands and the UK. She has since settled from the nomadic life and returned to Australia where she spends her time painting, making jewelry, and writing.

Tara has written for tabletop game publishers such as Angry Hamster Publishing, and previously contributed short stories to numerous magazines and newspapers in Australia and Europe. She has also previously frequented local pop culture and comic conventions where she sold her art and handcrafted costume accessories.

PAUL CAGGEGI
Artist
Australia

Instagram @pcaggegi
paulcaggegi.com
youtube.com/PaulOCaggegi

Paul is a first-generation Australian and son of Italian immigrants. He lives with his wife, a Vietnamese refugee, and their two daughters. Paul has worked in motion graphics, video editing, and 3D visual effects for almost twenty years. He lectured in design and 3D modeling at the JMC (John Martin Cass) Academy and now works with the RMK Crew. Paul has worked on projects ranging from TV commercials, web videos, showreels, and media packages. He has also done freelance work for prominent studios such as Nickelodeon, Saatchi & Saatchi, and Leo Burnett. Paul has since become a Blender ambassador, creating online tutorials and facilitating workshops worldwide.

Aside from his Blender expertise, Paul is best known online for one of his online comics: *Homebased*, which features comedic vignettes of everyday life as a stay-at-home dad.

HIS HEART IS MINE

I don't think the military fatigue was all for show. Along with the outfit, he had an intense gaze. Whether by military training or street toughness, he certainly conveyed that he could break a person in half, if he wanted. Yet, the unintentional pose was all too perfect. Sure, his heart might be physically on the other side, but the gesture, poetically, carried the same meaning. Without warning, she turned and gave him a big kiss on the cheek. He blushed uncontrollably and broke into the biggest and brightest smile I had seen all day.

JEROME WALFORD
Jamaica / United States

Instagram + Twitter   @forwardcomix
forwardcomix.com

THE PLAY BOY

"The face of a playboy is cynical. However, behind the mask of a smile, there might be a timid child crying and scared of everything." Li Zhang is currently a freelance illustrator based in New York City who is originally from China. She graduated from the Fashion Institute of Technology with a degree in illustration. Prior to moving to the States she worked as a product engineer for Groupe PSA in Shanghai. Combining rational logical thinking with creative imagination, she enjoys creating intricate, symbolic, geometrical illustrations that celebrate diversity and the power of storytelling through a colorful pattern-based style.

LI ZHANG
China / United States

Instagram @lizhangart
lizhangart.com

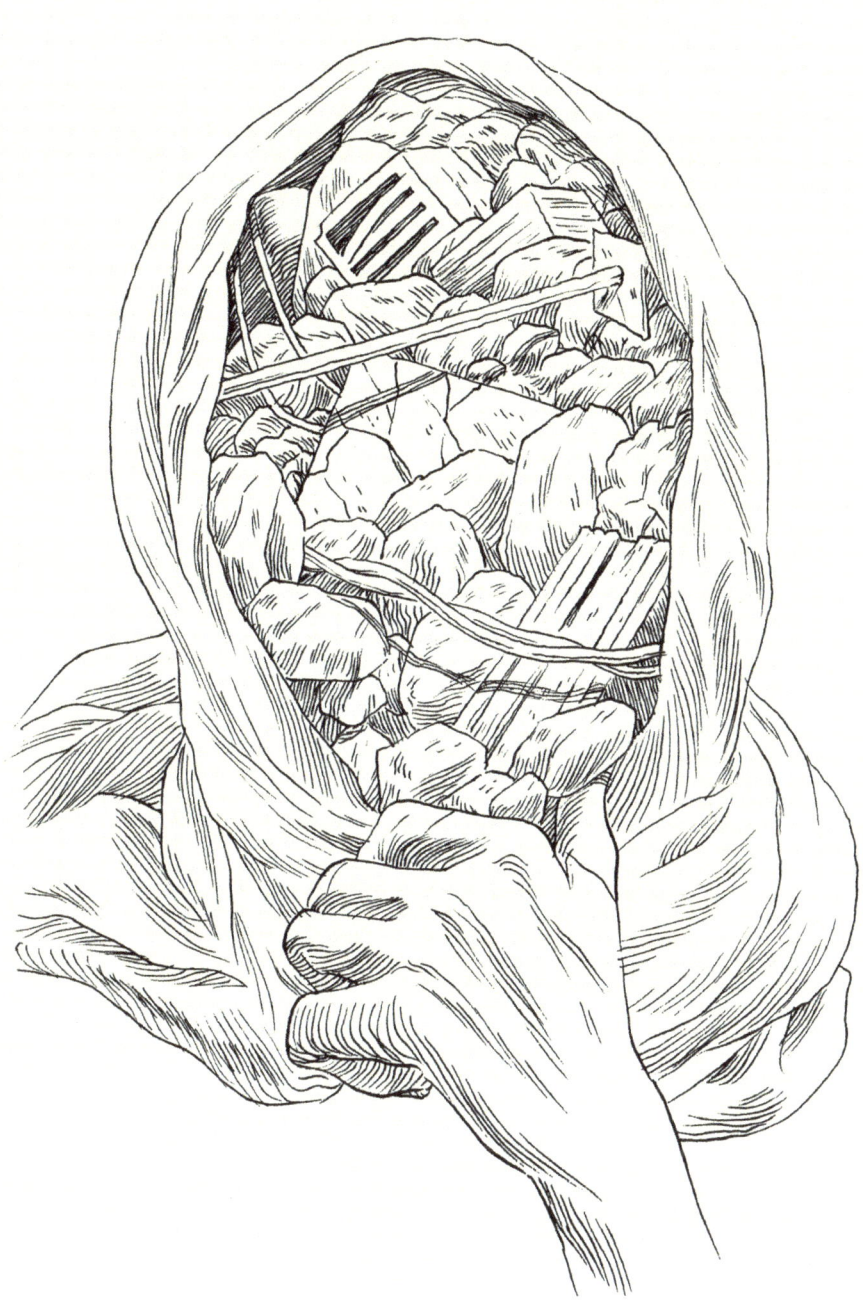

WITNESS

Anuj Shrestha is a cartoonist and illustrator. His comics have been listed in several editions of *The Best American Comics* anthology. His illustration work has appeared in *The New York Times*, *The New Yorker*, *McSweeney's*, *Playboy*, and *Wired*, among others. He currently resides in Philadelphia. *Witness* is from the series *Interiors*, a collection of drawings speaking to the experiences of refugees and immigrants surviving in areas of high conflict such as Palestine, Syria, Yemen, and others.

ANUJ SHRESTHA
United States

Instagram @anujink
anujink.com

TREE FACES
A central part of the human identity is our connection to the land of our birth, and if different, the land of our ancestors. Being willing to embrace the notion of struggle to find deep connection, while facing cycles of generational uprooting, is perhaps a helpful aspect to regaining a human connection.

Originally from Ridgewood, Queens, Leo now resides in New Britain, Connecticut. He's a graduate from the University of Hartford with a degree in Illustration, and also earned an Associate's degree in Fine Arts at Tunxis Community College. Aside from comics, Leo also creates whimsical illustrations that focus on nature, creatures, monsters, and ghouls.

LEONARDO GONZALEZ Instagram @lagonzart
United States

SUNFLOWERS
With a set of beautiful, hand-painted watercolor pieces, Kayla Walford, echoes the sub-theme of expressing the immigrant experience through interpretive nature portraits. Her delicate sunflower pieces reflect a sense of gentle confidence.

Kayla Walford is a young, emerging artist with a natural ability in water based art mediums. Along with exploring other artistic mediums, Kayla continues to practice and develop her skills in watercolors.

KAYLA WALFORD
United States

DAMIAN WAMPLER
Writer
United States

Damian Wampler was born and raised in Delaware, and earned a BA (Bachelor of Arts) in English and Anthropology from Boston University, and an MA in Russian and Central Asian Studies from UW-Madison. Damian began his art career in photography and playwriting, finding success when his play *Twin Towers* was accepted into New York City's Planet Connections Theater Festival in 2009. Damian's work as a fine art documentary photographer led to two images from his series *Darfur in Brooklyn* being purchased by the Brooklyn Museum and added to their permanent collection. Broken Icon Comics published Damian's first graphic novel, *Sevara*, in 2015. His short comic, *Kingdom of Ashes*, appeared in *Geometry Literary Magazine* in June 2019, and his second graphic novel, *Monitor*, will be published in spring 2020 by Broken Icon Comics. He also works as a U.S. diplomat stationed overseas at embassies and consulates.

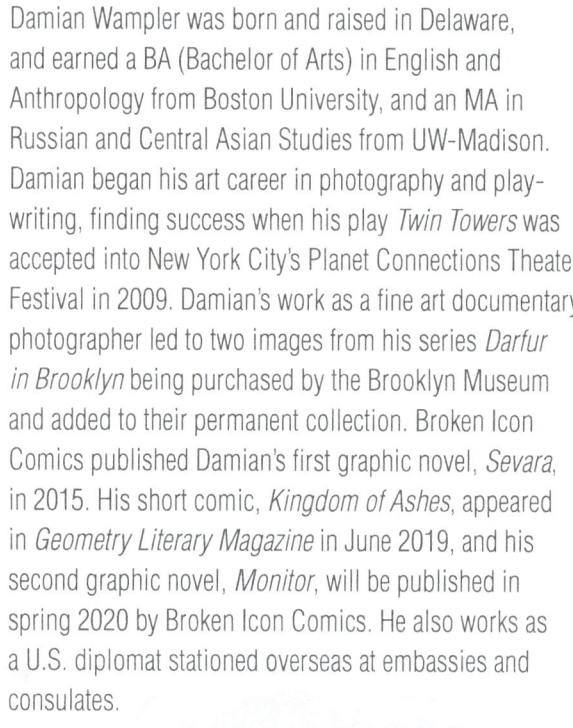

ELISABETH MKHEIDZE
Artist
Republic of Georgia

Elisabeth Mkheidze is a professional illustrator from the Republic of Georgia. Born and raised in Tbilisi, she has a BA (Bachelor of Fine Arts) in fine art from the Tbilisi State Academy of Arts and is currently enrolled there in a Restoration and Conservation Master's program. In 2015, she began working in the comic book industry and created her own fantasy series, *Irene's Eye*. She went on to work on the first indie comic published in Georgia called *Qarami*. In 2017, her story, *A Scorned Hero*, was selected to be part of Behemoth Comics' anthology, *Space Copz: Origins*. In 2019, she collaborated with American writer, Damian Wampler, to complete a sci-fi graphic novel, *Monitor,* which will be published by Broken Icon Comics in spring 2020. Her new graphic novel, *Golden Lion*, is in production with American creator Grant Freeman.

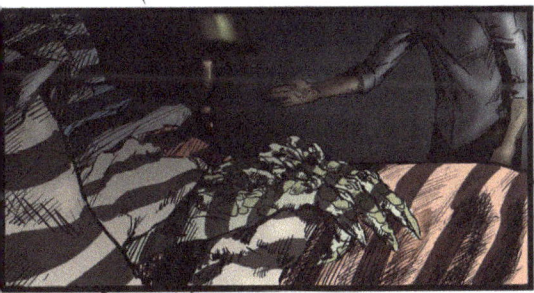

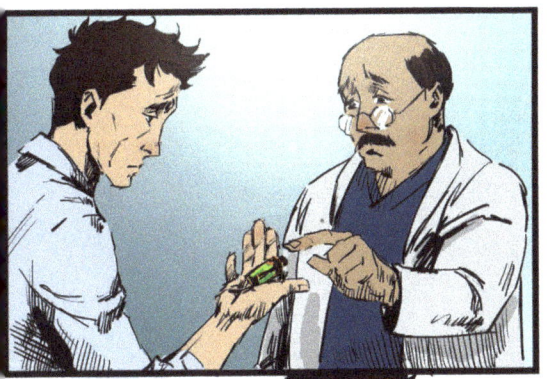

MATT YOCUM
Writer
United States / Middle East area

Matt Yocum is a Colonel in the U.S. Air Force with over twenty-six years of active military service. He has served as a mechanical engineer, an operations officer in special operations, and a Middle East area specialist stationed on multiple occasions in the region. He's written for Marvel Comics, and has a series currently in development with First Comics. When not conducting military duties or writing, he spends time with his family in North Carolina where he's currently stationed. Matt is hard at work on his next comic book series, *The Mankind War*, a labor of love he's developed over thirty years that culminates in a carefully designed future history in which all of his stories are set.

JOHN AMOR
Artist
The Philippines / United States

John Amor is an Eisner-nominated artist and writer from the Philippines. He has worked with Image, IDW, and Zuda Comics. He currently co-creates the Webtoon urban fantasy series *Urban Animal* with good friend, writer Justin Jordan. He is known for his accessible style and crisp storytelling. His artistic influences include Stuart Immonen, Mike Mignola, Mike Wieringo, and Greg Capullo. When not creating comics, John runs multiple *Dungeons & Dragons* campaigns in Davao, where he lives with his wife and two hounds.

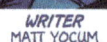

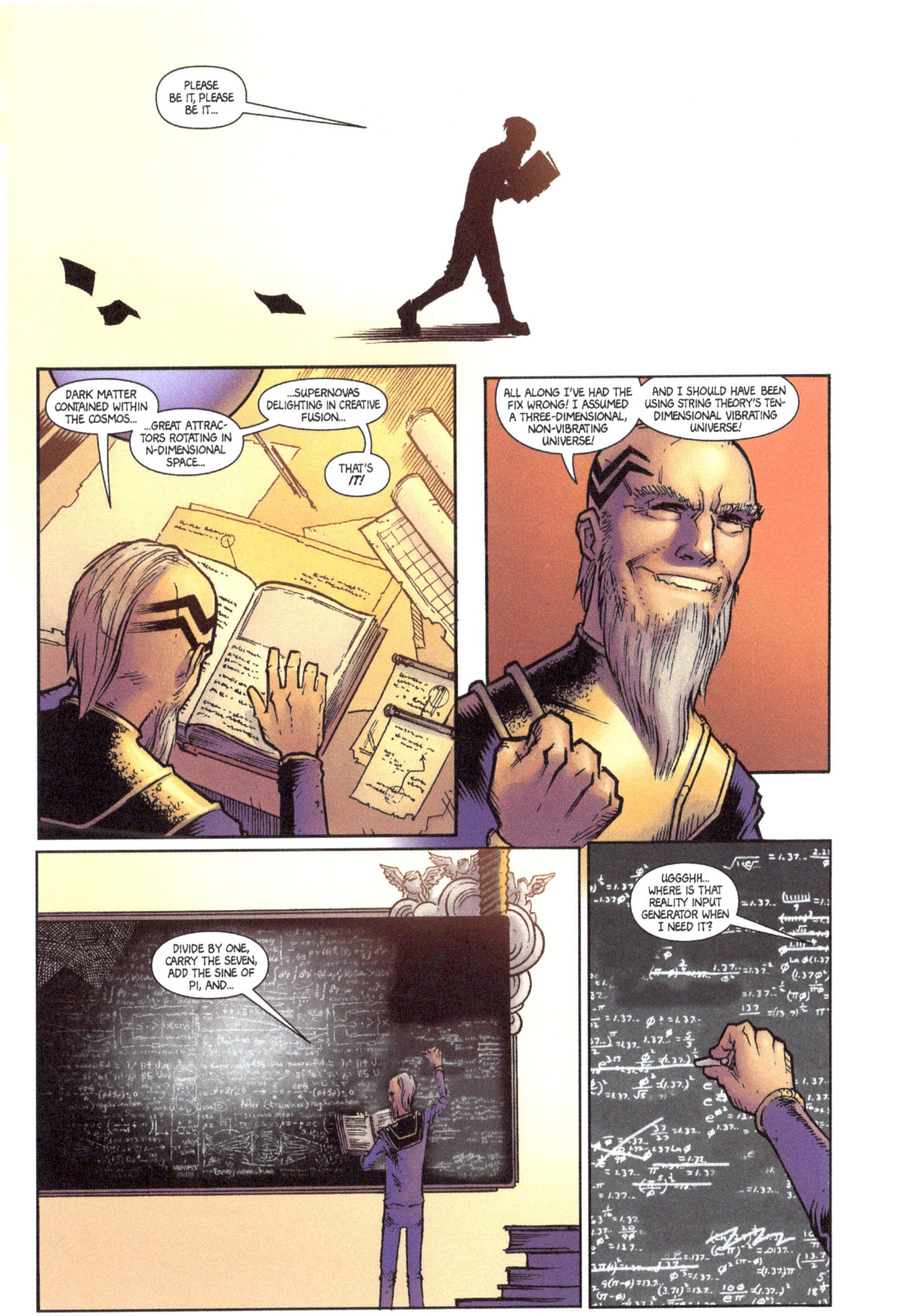

FOUR GENERATIONS OF CAWLEY

We celebrate the mothers who cross continents, foreign places, languages, and back again. We celebrate the passing of tradition and heritage through generations.

JULIA CAWLEY
United States / Germany
juliacawley.com

Little Swallow's Journey to Color

by Yan Gabriella

YAN GABRIELLA PEROPAT
Writer / Artist
China / United States

Instagram @ yangabriella
yangabriella.com

Yan Gabriella had just turned five when she received her first box of crayons and paper on a flight from China to America. This was not only a journey to her new home but also a journey to becoming an artist. In elementary school, she was introduced to art at the Children's Aid Society in their after-school programs. In high school, she attended Fiorello LaGuardia High School of Music & Art and Performing Arts, and finally, Yan received her BFA (Bachelor of Fine Arts) at the Maryland Institute College of Art. In addition to being a writer and illustrator, she also teaches what she has learned to children at The East End Arts Council. She is currently in the Art Education masters program at the School of Visual Arts in New York City.

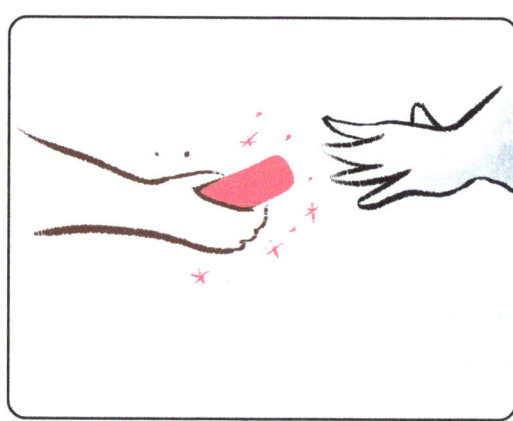
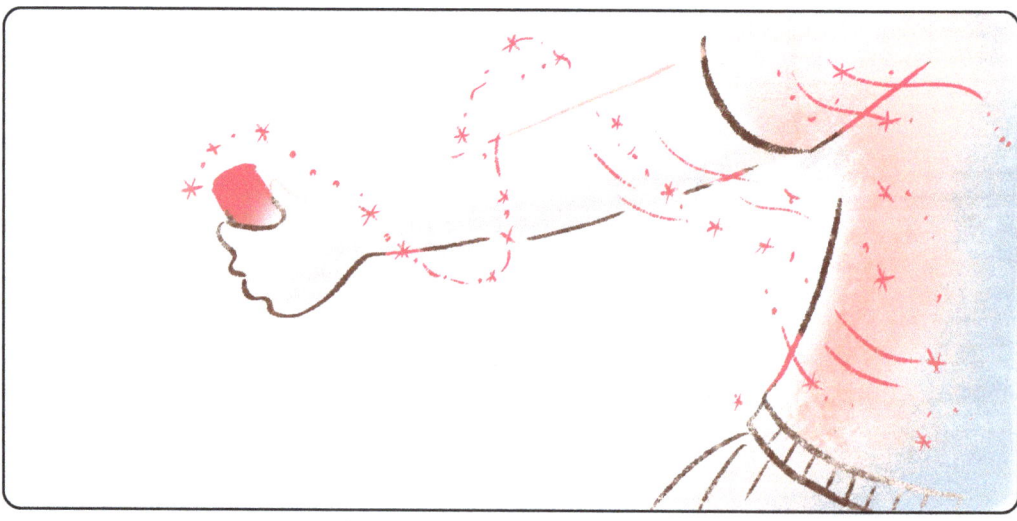

Xiǎo yàn zi, chuān huā yī
小燕子，穿花衣，
nián nián chūn tiān lái zhè lǐ
年年春天来这里，
wǒ wèn yàn zi nǐ wèi shá lái
我问燕子你为啥来，
yàn zi shuō
燕子说，
zhè lǐ de chūn tiān zuì měi lì
这里的春天最美丽。
Xiǎo yàn zi gào su nǐ
小燕子，告诉你，
jīn nián zhè lǐ gèng měi lì
今年这里更美丽。
huān yíng nǐ cháng qī zhù zài zhè lǐ.
欢迎你长期住在这里。

Little swallow,
so colorfully dressed,
comes here this spring.
I asked her,
"Why do you come here?"
She said,
"The spring here is the
most beautiful."
Little swallow, let me tell you,
it's more beautiful here this year.
Stay here with us forever.

Wang Li "Little Swallow"
Chinese Nursery Rhyme

100cameras is a nonprofit organization that works with kids around the world who have had challenging experiences, and teaches them how to process and tell their stories through photography.

During the spring of 2019, 100cameras joined in the work of an IDP (internally displaced persons) camp located in Khanke Village, Kurdistan, in Iraq. The kids we worked alongside were displaced Yazidi youth who fled when Islamic State fighters invaded and destroyed their home in Sinjar in 2014, forcing them to make a treacherous, weeks-long escape to safety – with thousands not surviving or being captured and forced into slavery.

Photo by Khalaf, Age 9 (2019)

100cameras provides a platform to sell their photographs, and gives 100 percent of the proceeds to fund the most pressing needs in their communities, enabling them to see the impact of their contribution.

With the reality that they have now been displaced and living in tents in an IDP camp through heat and snow, for over five years, and may never be able to return to their home due to the mass destruction, or even the trauma of such a return. **Our method utilizes photography as a powerful tool for self-expression, processing, and feeling ownership in the stories of their individual lives and those of their communities.** Our approach intentionally leaves the boundaries open and clear because it is their right to feel and share.

Visit us online to learn more about our work in Khanke, Iraq, and other locations.

100cameras
Khanke, Iraq
Instagram @100cameras
100cameras.org/flagship-khanke

RAMON GIL
Writer / Artist
The Philippines / United States

ramongil.com

Ramon Gil was born and raised in the Philippines and moved to the United States as a teen. He has been quite active in the Asian-American community, having organized the Asian Pacific American Heritage Festival in New York City for almost a decade, and published Asian in America Magazine online from 2003-2007. As a comic book writer and artist, he has been published by Vortex Comics, Dynamite Entertainment, Atlas Unleashed, Stache Publishing, Pronto Comics, and many more. Currently, he teaches art and comics at the Fashion Institute of Technology, where he also founded and runs Diversity Comic Con. In fall of 2019, he went back to school to earn his MFA (Masters of Fine Arts) in Illustration.

ERIK REEVES
Writer and Artist
United States

Instagram @Erikreevesart
erockalipse.deviantart.com

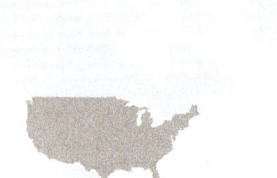

Artist: *Hoodratz In Space, Peacekeeper, Throwd* comic series; Concept Artist: *Transformers: War for Cybertron* video Game; Sketchcard Artist: *Marvel Now, Iron Man 3, Guardians of the Galaxy, Marvel Premiere*

Erik Reeves worked as a concept artist in video games for companies including THQ, Activision, and Blizzard. He has worked as a penciler, inker, and writer on several independent comics for companies such as Image Comics, Antarctic Press, and Viper comics. He is currently working as a sketchcard artist for Marvel and Upperdeck Entertainment while self-publishing his Kickstarter funded *Hoodratz In Space* comic series and more...

Erik grew up, like so many, a victim of a broken marriage, without a mother to help guide him in a world of so many different paths.

Cut off from many family members spread out in different states, it's a real honest contrast to being an immigrant living within the United States.

Disconnected from a stable family life, Erik found himself creating worlds that reflect his outlook on survival in today's modern society.

Like his fan page on Facebook, and follow him on Twitter and Instagram.

ERIK REEVES'
HOODRATZ IN SPACE

STARDUST

SOMEWHERE IN SPACE...

SEEDS FOR A NEW NUBIAN EMPIRE

CJ came up with the idea of Abyssinia Media Group 1996 under the name Abyssinia Comic Group, while employed as the art director for Africa World Press /The Red Sea Press, Inc. The concept was to tell African-centered stories for a school populace that was learning about their African cultural roots in comic book format. The featured cover illustration begins a story within the franchise, *Ayele Nubian Warrior*, in which the title villain begins the prologue to the story.

CARLES (CJ) JUZANG
United States

facebook.com/AbyssiniaMedia.net
Instagram @abyssinia_media_group

THE FORGE AT ILE-IFE
The amalgamation of African cultures sets the stage for an epic adventure, told through the eyes of Malika. As the Empire of Azzaz and the Ming Dynasty clash, breathtaking fantastical elements (magic, relics, and dragons) are introduced via ancient mythological artifacts and beings called the Divine Ones. This image shows Malika journeying to an ancient site where the Divine Ones once lived.
Art by Godwin Akpan.

ROYE OKUPE / YOUNEEK STUDIOS
Lagos, Nigeria / United States
Instagram @ youneekstudios
youneekstudios.com

HOSTAGES OF THE SPHERE

This moving, Afro-futuristic piece displays the enduring importance of family, and the potential lingering effects of refugee crises and displacement. Eric is a professional Illustrator who has worked in film, commercials, video games, and the publishing industry for nearly twenty years. His client list includes Activision, Disney Publishing, Scholastic, Random House, Upper Deck, and Weta Workshop. He has taught in the illustration department at Syracuse University, and guest-lectured at Syracuse University's Visual Communication Symposium, the Fashion Institute of Technology, and for classes at The School of Visual Arts NYC.

ERIC WILKERSON
United States

ericwilkersonart.com
ericwilkerson.blogspot.com

GODDESS OF FERTILITY

My sister is a part of me. One of the things I'm most thankful for in this life is the bond I share with her. Watching her create life was both horrifying and beautiful. It's hard to see someone you love so much experience the pain of pregnancy and childbirth, but beautiful and inspiring to see them level up and come into their own as a mother.

HILLARY WILSON
United States

Instagram @hillarydwilsonart
hdwilsonart.com

GLADIIS

My name is Okera Damani, a citizen of Trinidad and Tobago. I am a creator and my primary skill is 3D design/art. I graduated with a diploma in animation studies from the University of Trinidad and Tobago, and also received a certificate of completion from the AnimSchool in the United States. This enabled me to work closely with lecturers from studios like Disney and Dreamworks, who mentored me through the course of my projects.

The goal of this particular piece, titled "Gladiis" (part of a series) was to experiment with a mix between 2D illustration and 3D rendering. It's an effort to create a mural printed/painted kind of aesthetic. Like most artwork it visually expresses how I felt at the moment, accompanied along with the music I listened to while creating the piece. "Gladiis" shows an individual expressing himself to the fullest, as he is free and able to appear how he wishes, and is not confined to the standards of society. The initial caption of this piece read, "I know who I am and that's all that matters."

OKERA DAMANI
Trinidad and Tobago

Instagram @okera_
artstation.com/okera

What's In A Name
by Leah Yael Levy

> So nice to meet you!
>
> What's your name?

LEAH YAEL LEVY
Writer / Artist
Israel / United States

leahyaellevy.com

Leah Yael Levy is a visual artist, storyteller, and teacher based in Berkeley, California.
She was born and raised in Moshav Beit Lechem Haglilit, Israel. She first moved to New York City in 2002 to attend the Art Students League of New York, and later gained a BFA (Bachelor of Fine Arts) in Illustration from Parsons the New School for Design (2011). After four years creating visuals for The Unemployed Philosophers Guild (Brooklyn), she moved to California to pursue an MFA in Comics at California College of the Arts (2017).

She is currently a Teaching Artist for Kala, the Richmond Art Center and the Jewish Community Center (JCC) of the East Bay. Her work has been published by Forward Comix (2017) and *The Nib* (2018) as well as self-published.

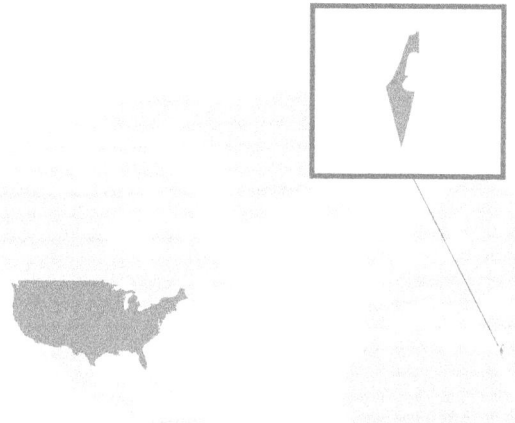

יעל

It's also a character from the Bible

"She's not actually even of the Israelites; she's from a neighboring tribe."

"But she helps them win a war."

"She invites the commander of the enemy's army into her tent and gives him warm milk."

²⁴"Most blessed of women be Jael, the wife of Heber the Kenite, most blessed of tent-dwelling women. ²⁵He asked for water, and she gave him milk; in a bowl fit for nobles she brought him curdled milk. ²⁶Her hand reached for the tent peg, her right hand for the workman's hammer. She struck Sisera, she crushed his head, she shattered and pierced his temple. ²⁷At her feet he sank, he fell; there he lay. At her feet he sank, he fell; where he sank, there he fell—dead.

"Then she murders him in his sleep with a tent peg."

²⁸Through the window peered Sisera's mother; behind the lattice she cried out, 'Why is his chariot so long in coming? Why is the clatter of his chariots delayed?' The wisest of her ladies answer her; indeed, she keeps saying to herself, 'Are they not finding and dividing the spoils: a woman or two for each man, colorful garments as plunder for Sisera, colorful garments embroidered, highly embroidered garments for my neck— all this as plunder?' So may all your enemies perish, Lord! But may all who love you be like the sun when it rises in its strength. Then the land had peace forty years."

~ Deborah's Song ~
Judges , 5

Occasionally, a Catholic person knows this story. Most Americans I've met have never really read the Bible.

With time, I have come to use Leah in professional settings, my website and work email both use my full name, so people who have only met me digitally often think my name is Leah.

"I've heard that name before"

"Are you ISRAELI?"

"Hi, Leah!"

"Hey uh... You can actually call me Yael"

"Oh, cool"

"Ya- How?"

"YA-EL"

"What kind of name IS THAT?"

"Umm— I mean"

"Where are you from?"

Back home, Yael is one of those names, like Mary or Jane over here. In school, whenever someone called "YAEL!" at least three girls would turn around. Leah was like an old lady's name though. I had two (maybe three?) teachers named Leah.

So I only started using it after moving to the States. Mostly in situations when I didn't want to get into a conversation about it, like at a coffee shop. And with people who REALLY can't pronounce Yael.

Leah is such a common name, people here can all say it, they usually even know how to spell it.

"Can I have a name for your order?"

"Leah"

"So where am I from?"

"It depends how far you go."

"I live in California."

"I was born in Israel."

"My Dad was also born in Israel."

"His parents came from Yemen."

"My mom was born in New York."

"Her dad came from Russia (Ukraine) and her mom's family came from Poland."

"So basically I'm a mutt."

"Wanna talk about my hair next?"

It was my American grandfather Jerry who insisted the name Leah be my first name.

Jerry had been trying for years to have each grandchild born before me to be somehow named after his mother Leah, or Lilian.

My mom says more than one of my cousins has a second name that starts with L

For my cousin Kendra, Leah is like her Hebrew name

Only I got it as a first name.

Though it started out as a second name, and ended up doubling as my American name.

"It's REALLY important to me!"

"I don't know, daddy"

"We finally decided on Yael"

"It's fine. It's just a piece of paper"

"We'll call her Yael"

I was actually Mic'hal (even harder to pronounce!) for a few days, before my mom changed her mind.

It's funny, Leah is a much more common name universally, really. Yet it is actually the piece of my name that sets me apart from THOUSANDS of people named *Yael Levy*.

I don't know of even one other *Leah Yael Levy* out there. So my grandpa's stubbornness actually helped make my name more unique.

His stubborness may have ultimately helped me out in more than one way.

"It's nice to have the choice to opt out. If I'm not in the mood to talk about where I come from or how you spell my name,"

"I can just be Leah."

"But if you ever really get to know me, you'll know I am Yael."

THE TOMB SWEEPERS

BY DANIEL HOM

DAN HOM
Writer
United States

danhom.com

Daniel is a hobbyist writer and blogger. Imagine him as the kid next door who randomly disappears, talking about "wanting to see the world or something," only to come back telling stories so mundane and weird you wonder if he left at all. Now imagine that but ten times less glamorous.

He blogs about life: its quirks, its jokes, its ups and downs. More recently, he's been writing about taking care of his parents through aging, Alzheimer's, and even death. This is when he's not too lazy to write in the first place.

He lives in the San Francisco Bay Area. He's a proud son, little brother, and uncle.

1

He's just a child, but like all children of the world, he can see ghosts—ghosts of the past, ghosts of ancient tradition, ghosts of things he does not yet understand.

The ghost he knows best is the ghost of his grandmother. He recognizes her, though he has never met her. He has only ever seen her in pictures, but in the world of the living, pictures are enough.

She is his mother's mother, and he knows that she is a woman who loved his mother dearly. He also knows this, through pictures of the past—the past where the two of them are together, and the two of them are happy.

He's just a child, but even in naiveté, he can sense that his mother is truly happy in only one place: those pictures of the past.

He wonders if that's why his mother so often takes him to his grandmother's tomb—she misses her mother, she wants to see her, and her ghost is always there, eagerly awaiting their arrival. Rain or shine. Freezing or sweltering. It matters not. She is always there, immune to the elements, and immune to time.

When they visit, the child follows his mother's lead, cleaning his grandmother's tombstone, picking up the leaves and branches, brushing the dirt aside, placing a fresh bunch of flowers—bright shades of red, yellow, green, purple—his mother always chooses the brightest shades.

And then she opens her mouth; she speaks. The child is young, and he does not always understand the sounds. He does not always understand the words. But he does not need to understand either, to understand that the two of them—mother, and ghost—are, for a moment, together again.

2

The child's mother is a Tomb Sweeper, chosen to carry the traditions of her ancestors, chosen to carry the traditions that allow her—and others like her—to commune with their ancestors.

As her son, the child too is chosen, and it is from his mother that he is also meant to learn how to commune with the ghosts of generations past. He is studious, and quick to learn, but he cannot learn what his mother does not teach, and there are traditions she does not teach him to follow, because they are the traditions she does not follow herself.

Those traditions would have remained a mystery to the child, remnants of an era that would have been lost in the past, but tradition has powerful allies in Death and Time. Death is a constant, and Time often continues to carry those things we often wish it would leave behind.

When Death comes for his paternal grandfather, the child and his family travel a far distance, to a land that Legend once proclaimed: "If you can make it here, you can make it anywhere."

It is here, in a dark room, where the child joins more than fifty others—all of them bound by blood, all of them Tomb Sweepers—ready to release his grandfather from the world of the living.

It is in a dark room, lit by a distant pit of fire, where the child suddenly senses many other beings—all of them ghosts, all of them his ancestors—ready to receive his grandfather into the realm of their world.

It is in this dark room, that the child suddenly realizes that there are other tomb sweeping traditions—others that belong to generations and generations before him, others that he does not know.

There is the burning of wooden sticks. The sticks are pungent, and the child does not like the smell of them.

There is the burning of paper—money—a symbol of hope for wealth in the next life. The child remembers he was taught to not love money.

And then, there is the thing that the Tomb Sweepers do, in unison, something which nearly frightens the child.

They bow.

Four people break tradition. A cousin, and the child's family—his mother, his father, and his older brother.

The child begins to panic. He does not know whom to follow. He does not have the years needed to understand the choice he is about to make. He only knows to follow his instincts, instincts which tell him to follow his mother, the queen—and king—of his family.

The room bows again. Five people do not.

The child does not fear ghosts; what he fears most is disappointment—disappointment from the ghosts, disappointment from the others in the room. He senses that there was a right way to do things, that he chose not to follow it, instead choosing to follow his mother as one of the five who stay on their feet as all others fall to their knees.

The child speaks quietly to himself. He hopes his mother will reward his obedience. He hopes his mother will shield him from the others.

He hopes that the ghosts he sees—and the disappointment he feels—are merely figments of his imagination, and that they are not actually there.

3

There are things in this world that can be studied, but cannot truly be learned unless they are taught—and although Experience is not always the best teacher, it is often, the only teacher.

When Death comes again, this time for the child's remaining grandfather, his mother's father, the child's mother leaves for the land of her childhood, a fragrant harbor that Legend once proclaimed was where East and West collided, and she asks her child to come with her.

By now, he is already no longer quite a child in body, but still quite a child in mind. He is studious, but rebellious; hardworking, but shortsighted. And like all children, he begins to develop his own ideas of the world, and he begins to fight back. He has the foolishness to ask to stay home. He is worried about many things. He is worried about failing his studies, about competing against his peers, he is worried about his future—all things the Future, in fact, cares little for.

He also has the naiveté to do what he is told.

The child's family arrives in time to see his grandfather, but not in time to commune with him, to speak to him and learn the wisdom and ways of the past. Instead, the child is granted a separate gift. He is in the land where his mother once lived, and as if he is also a Time Traveler, the child spends his days experiencing his mother's past with his mother as his guide—the food she ate, the place she lived, the people she knew. If he were older, if he had the words, he would say he felt connected to her in a way he had never before. He would say that knowing her traditions, is to know her.

He would also say that he does not want to go home. He knows that once he leaves—with his mother's father now gone—he will never be asked to come back. And return home they must, and when they do, they bury the child's grandfather next to his grandmother, intertwining the point in time and space that connects their physical bodies and their ghostly ones, reuniting the two souls which had been separated for many, many years.

The child's mother visits often. She misses her mother and father, she wants to see them. And when they visit, the child follows his mother's lead, cleaning the tombstone, picking up the leaves and branches, brushing the dirt aside, placing a fresh bunch of flowers—still in the brightest shades.

And then she lowers her head, folds her hands, and she begins to speak. By now, the child is old enough to understand the sounds, old enough to understand the words. He is finally old enough to understand that his mother is beginning to pray—pray to a being she gives the name God, a being she believed died on a Cross, Our Father who art in heaven.

But the child is also old enough now to know that something is wrong. His mother is a Tomb Sweeper. So is he. They are chosen. They cannot not be one. This leaves him questioning. He does not understand the tradition of the Cross to believe in ghosts, and he does not understand the tomb sweeping tradition to believe in a heavenly father.

Still, he holds his questions and hides them in his heart, as he once again follows his mother, bowing his head, folding his hands. He will not openly question her. He cannot.

He has only studied the traditions of the world.

She has lived them.

4

To raise a child is to wrestle with paradox. Mothers and fathers raise children so that they no longer are in need of mothers and fathers. And yet, with their job complete, mothers and fathers are often unable to let their children go, to let them be any-thing other than children in need of mothers and fathers.

This is what the child learns as he grows and grows, until one day he leaves his home in search of the world, as all children do.

He is a fortunate child, born in the land of the free and the home of the brave, a land where he is free to pursue things beyond food, water, shelter—free to pursue his own path.

But freedom can be lonely, and the child leaves his home only because it is expected of him, and not because he is brave enough to choose it for himself.

He finds that the world is in fact, a universe. At first this excites the child, and he gathers questions upon questions, eager to discover the boundaries of knowledge.

But questions are heavy, and the universe is big, and even bigger still. It is not long before the child becomes lost, tired, and unsure of which way to turn, other than to return to the things he knows.

He starts with his mother's God, though when he tries to find Him, he is unsuccessful.

He tries to find others who call themselves Tomb Sweepers, though when he does, he finds their traditions foreign, and he is left wondering if he is even a Tomb Sweeper at all.

He asks others how to commune with ghosts. Not everyone is willing to share. Not everyone believes in ghosts.

He speaks to his mother about this, who shows disdain for his many questions. She does not see the point. In her many years, she has seen that the world spins a certain way that does not change.

Death is a constant. Time is relative. God is the holiest of ghosts. She tells him all this, as she always has.

"You don't understand, Jai," she calls him.

He bristles at the word. He tells her that he is not a child anymore.

But he is. His mother will always worry for him, because he is her child. That is her role, and roles are difficult to bend, and even more difficult to break.

He slowly begins to understand that his mother is not a constant, that his mother, herself, is changing under the influence of Time. He slowly begins to understand that nobody is truly free from connection, free from the past—that we are all born of something, and that just as he will always be a child to his mother, his mother was once a child too, and in someone's eyes, will always be one.

He slowly begins to understand that his mother does not have all the answers because she once asked her own questions, because she once chose how she would live as a Tomb Sweeper, even if those choices were at odds with what came before. The child decides that he must do the same. He decides that he must also be brave, that he must learn to trust his own instincts, that he must confront that which he fears—disappointment, from the past, from the world, from his mother, from her God, from himself.

And so he does. He runs headfirst into the world that is in fact, a universe. He allows himself his questions, searches far and wide for answers. He challenges other Tomb Sweepers about their ways. He once again becomes a Time Traveler, connecting to his mother's past in the land of her childhood.

And then he decides to return to the land where he once felt disappointment from his Tomb Sweeping ancestors—he returns to the land of his paternal grandfather.

5

With the help of his remaining family, the child finds the tombs of his ancestors, those who carried what would become his future from the land of the middle kingdom to the land of the golden mountain, from the east of the expanse to the concrete jungle where dreams are made of.

Among those ancestors he finds his grandfather—the ghost of his grandfather. He remembers the dark room, the releasing of his grandfather from the world of the living. He remembers the pungent sticks, the burning of paper. He remembers the ghosts he sensed back then, the same as the ghosts he sees right now.

And he can see them watching him.

His remaining family knows of his hesitation. They know of his love and obedience to tradition, but they also know of his love and obedience to his mother. The two of those should be one, but they are not, and it is up to him to choose how he will hold the two together.

"You don't have to bow, you know," his aunt speaks to him. It is a stroke of kindness, of understanding, and he takes the words to heart.
He understands: It is his choice.

He thinks of his mother. He thinks of what she might say. He thinks of her impending disappointment.

He closes his eyes, and he bows.

When he opens his eyes, he is not struck down, as he once imagined he might have been.

He turns to his family, who are neither pleased, nor disappointed; they are too busy being Tomb Sweepers themselves.

He turns to the other ghosts, the ghosts of his ancestors. He asks if they were disappointed, those many years ago, and they nod. He asks if they are pleased now, and they nod.

They do not speak to him, but their nodding is enough; he now understands that they were disappointed then, and pleased now, not because of whether he chose to bow, to follow their tradition. They are pleased because he chose to learn about their traditions.

They are pleased because he chose to remember them.

6

Word travels fast, and word travels far.

Although he is a great distance from home, the child has gotten word that Death has come for his father's mind. He has gotten word that Death has begun to take pieces of his mother's body. He has gotten word, that his mother has begun to prepare her own tomb.

This brings the child home, and he finds that his home is foreign, and very different from the home he left. He finds that home, is not really home at all.
He finds that his mother still clings to her God, though something about her belief has changed, something he cannot quite explain.

He finds that his father is weak. His father remembers few things. He does not laugh and joke and move the way he used to. He is not a ghost, but he is already beginning to act like one.

He finds that his mother wants to care for his father, and though she will not admit it, he finds that she cannot do it alone.

"Why don't you get more help?" the child asks his mother, knowing that he, himself, is also not enough.

"No, this is my job," his mother rejects him, "you don't understand, Jai." The child does not relent. He openly questions her now, but because he is open with his questions, it also means that he is open to her.

He tells her that he has left her God behind. This saddens her, but he remains obedient, and kind, and remains supportive of her beliefs. And so she is happy.

He tells her that he has learned of the traditions she has tried to hide from him, that he has discovered many other ways of a world that is in fact, a universe. This confuses her, but she sees that he is happy, and what else do mothers and fathers want, than to see their children happy.

He tells her that he will stay to help her follow her God, that he will stay to help her take care of his father.

He tells her that he will stay to help her prepare her tomb, the tomb she had begun preparing for many years now, the point in time and space that will one day connect her physical body to her ghostly one. He tells her that he does not like this, he tells her that it frightens him, that he is not ready for her to become a ghost. But by choosing to stay, he also tells her that he loves her, that he will carry her tradition, and that he will carry her.

She smiles at him when he tells her this. He smiles back.

For a moment, like in the pictures of the past, she is happy again.

It is only for a moment, because Death does indeed come for the child's mother. Sooner than she was ready. Sooner, than he was ready.

7

In the child's studies, he discovered a word that looks like this: 孝
He knows its pronunciation as haau, or xiao, as others call it. It is a pictograph of a child supporting the elderly 老.

That is the word's meaning. Love. It means to love.

8

Time moves forward, but time also repeats itself, carrying forward what was left behind.

By now, the child is no longer truly a child; he has not been a child for many years. But even though he is a grown man, when he is with his mother, he knows he will always be—in some shape or form—a child.

He often goes to his mother's tomb, as often as he can, to the point in time and space that connects his mother's physical body to her ghostly one. It is the tomb she prepared for herself; it is the tomb he helped prepare with her.

He misses her. He wants to see her, and her ghost is always there, eagerly awaiting his arrival. Finding success or failure. Following her path, or his. It matters not. She is always there. She will always be there.

When he visits, he follows his memories as a child, cleaning his mother's tombstone, picking up the leaves and branches, brushing the dirt aside, placing a fresh bunch of flowers—bright shades of red, yellow, green, purple—he has inherited his mother's love for the brightest shades.

And then he opens his mouth; he speaks. He prays, following the prayers of his mother, her God, Our Father who art in heaven, even if he no longer believes in it.

But there are things he now follows not because he believes in them, but because he believes in their power to connect him to those who came before.

And so he also bows. He bends his knees. He vows to one day find those sticks, those strips of paper, those additional tomb sweeping traditions, so that he can remember and honor his past, all of it.

"I'm hungry," he remembers some of his mother's last words. "Can I have chicken? How about chicken?"

So he brings her chicken—fried chicken, a modern corruption of an older tomb sweeping tradition, but he does not care. It is his way of sharing a meal with her ghost; it is his way of honoring that tradition, of honoring her memory.

"How is it?" he asks, taking a bite himself.

"Good. Very good," she says, as she has always said. "You should have brought more."

The two of them share a laugh.

He tells her about his father. His brother. His brother's family. The others in the world of the living.

He listens to her speak, and though he cannot always understand her sounds, her words, he understands her smile, her spirit, the gentle lift that underscores every move she makes—just as he did when he was just a child. For a moment, the two of them are together, again.

And when he leaves her, promising to return again, he feels no guilt. He knows what he has left behind. He knows what he has embraced. If there are ghosts of disappointment, he does not see them, and they cannot touch him.

Because the child followed elements of what his mother wanted, elements of what tradition wanted, and then he combined them, which is what he wanted.

He is, after all, born into tradition. He is chosen. He is a Tomb Sweeper, and he cannot not be one; he can, however, choose what it does mean, to be one.

And that is a tradition he will pass down, to whomever follows him.

OUR BODIES BECAME RICE

MICHAEL WATSON
Artist
United States

Instagram @michaelwatsonart
mdwart.com

Michael Watson is a New York-based, Filipino-American artist who engages in experimental processes and alternative materials that are often extreme, interactive, and tied to specific sites, cultural experiences, and rituals, to create visceral mixed media panels, sculptures, installations, and performances. Through his work, Watson explores the space between being, substance, and imperceptibility through the use of rice and other materials as a substitute for the body. He received his MFA from Parsons School of Design and BFA from the Art Academy of Cincinnati. His exhibitions and residencies include B.W.A.C., NYC, stART Space Gallery, Manchester Center, Vermont, LaBodega Gallery, New York City, Hunterdon Art Museum, New Jersey, Sheila C. Johnson Design Center, NYC, Brooklyn Museum, New York City, Leila Heller Gallery, NYC, SOMArts Cultural Center, San Francisco, The Kitchen, New York City, Arts, Letters and Numbers, Averill Park, NY, AIR Program 4heads Org., NYC, the New York Studio Program, and the ChaShaMa Studio Program, New York City.

Growing up in a Filipino-American home, rice was a staple of every meal. Our bodies became rice. In my work, rice replaces conventional figures as a representation of the body. It provides a conceptual framework for exploring topics such as death, the afterlife, and interconnectivity.

The burn work is created through a unique charring technique I developed. I arrange rice and found objects on wood panels and burn them into the surface. The remaining afterimages capture the collision between life and death and point toward something deeper, beyond our physical boundaries and perceptions.

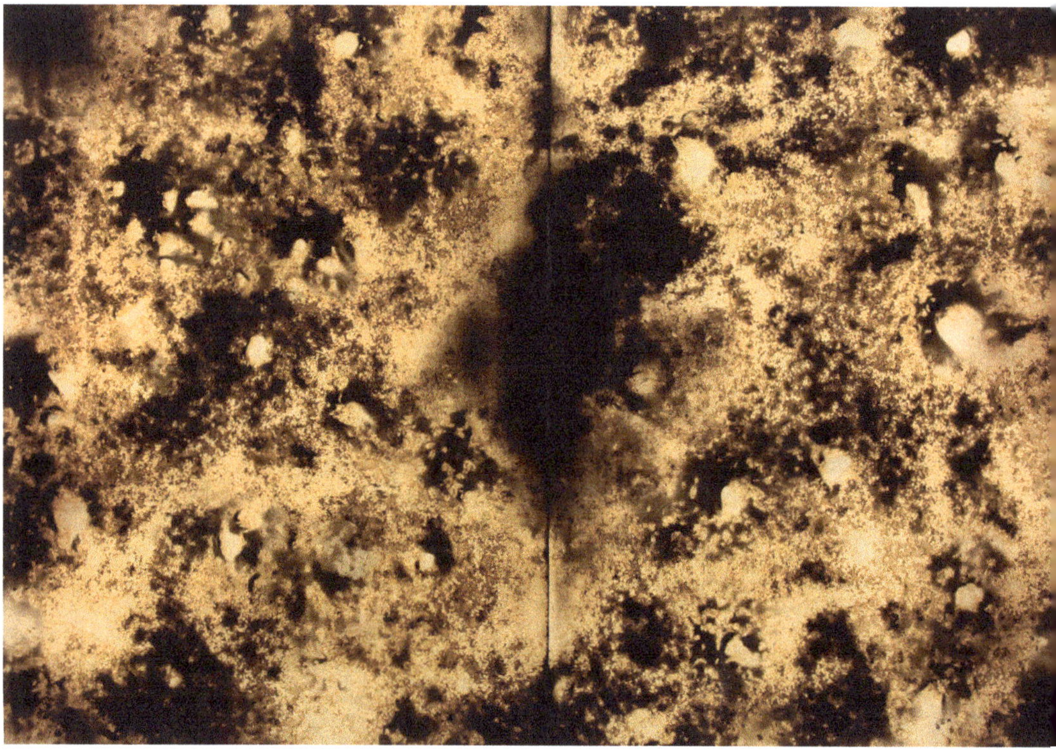

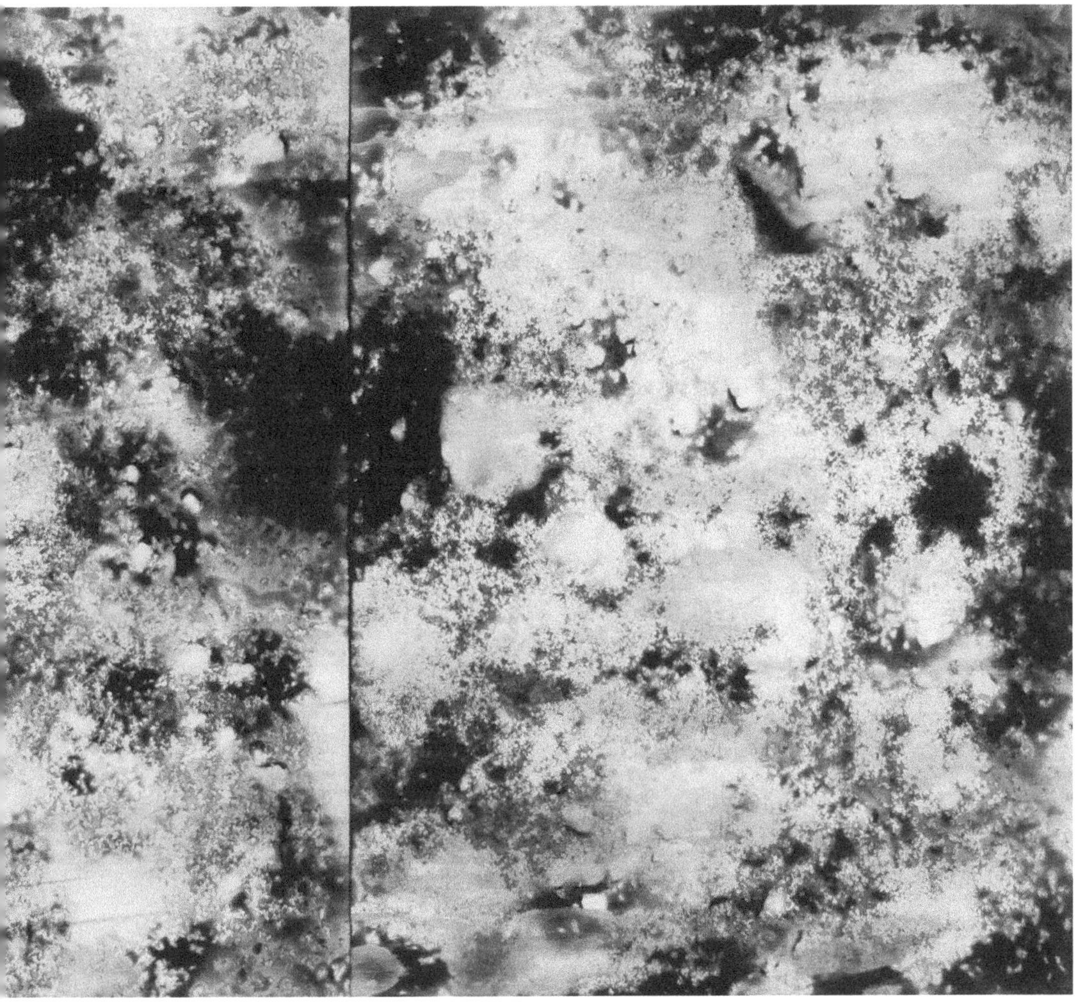

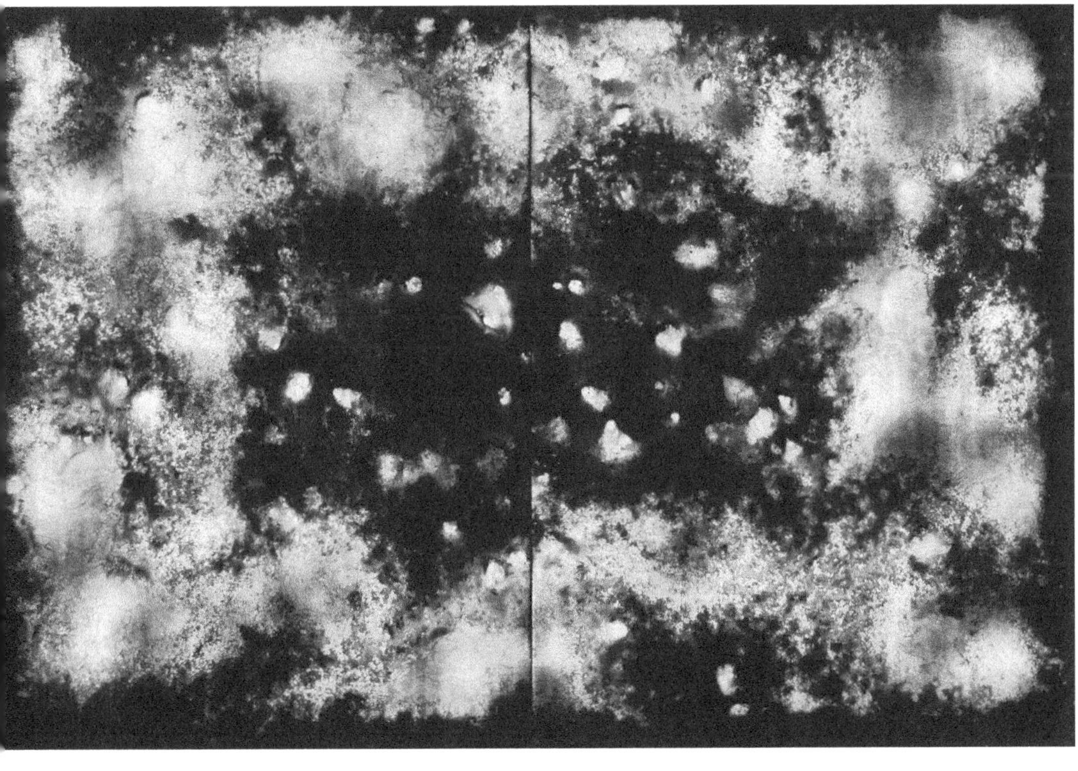

THE FOX

My name is Jasmine Haomin Shi. I am an illustrator currently studying at the School of Visual Arts in New York City. I am originally from Shanghai, China, so I like to add Chinese elements into my illustrations. One of my favorite things to draw is Asian mythological creatures. In the drawing of the fox, I illustrated a fox looking at a mysterious shrine far in the distance. It is an experimental piece for me — using traditional silkscreen techniques. I used color separations to create the feeling of depth of field and tried to maintain a limited color palette.

JASMINE HAOMIN SHI
China / United States

jazzzydrill.com/jasminehaominshi
Instagram: @jazzz_shm

GRADUATION

I recently graduated from the Illustration program at The School of Visual Arts (SVA). My mediums are etching, monoprints, and ink drawing – making editions of fine art prints. This piece is an etching done on a zinc plate and printed on paper. The piece was meant to illustrate how I felt while waiting on stage during graduation – I was overwhelmed and nervous at the time. The monsters symbolized my anxiety of being in this world. I currently freelance in New York City, working in a printmaking shop as a printer. I hope to someday establish my own printmaking studio in China.

ZHEYU WANG
China / United States

Instagram: @drinklinger
Website: jazzzydrill.com/aboutdrillinger
professor26rothchild@gmail.com

POTLUCK BOUNTY

Have you ever gone to a potluck at the home of a recent immigrant family? In my experience, there are many dishes that are foreign yet familiar. Sometimes there are items that obviously need to be prepared. Grab a plate and fill it up, but roll up your sleeves too; there's joyful work to be done.

JEROME WALFORD Instagram + Twitter @forwardcomix
Jamaica / United States forwardcomix.com

Some slaves will Never be slaves, And One Woman will Never be Conquered.

NANNY!

By Mervyn McKoy
Cover colors Inkfable
Special Thanks: Nicki McKoy

MERVYN MCKOY
Writer / Artist
Jamaica / United States

Instagram @paperlabstudios
paperlabstudios.com

Mervyn McKoy is a Jamaican storyteller, illustrator, and co-founder of Paper Lab Studios. McKoy has crafted artwork and concepts professionally for fifteen years, but many more if you count his poor parent's walls and school note books. He's had the pleasure of creating the titular Florida Supercon mascot "Lil' Herc" as well as providing sequentials on comics for Terminus Media, Paula Peril and the CDC (yes, that CDC).

McKoy is also the co-creator of the Kickstarter fan favorite and actual funny, funny books, *Giant Robot Warrior Maintenance Crew* (or *GRWMC* for short) and *The C -Listers*. When he's not hunkered down in the sequential trenches, he's working on parody art projects that have been both praised and lampooned by Destructoid, IGN, The Comedy Button and Conan O'Brien.

His most recent project, *Child of the Sun*, is available on Comixology and Amazon, while his next projects, 'Dogwald the Warrior', 'Speeders INC.' and 'Nanny!' are currently on the horizon.

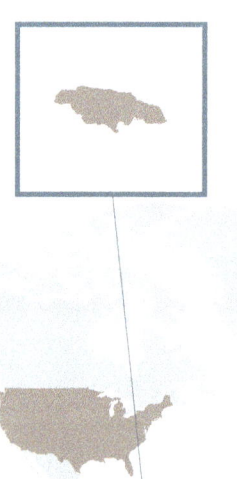

<You have already endured a horrific journey here. Believe me, I understand! True comfort I cannot offer.>

OKYEAME BODUA

COUGH

HELP!?

<I will not be accompanying you. I need to make sure we are not followed.>

IMORI 'ABA' ORI

WHER'S EVR'YON' D'WE WIN?

M-I DYIN'...

...WHY'S SO MUCH BLOOD?

LIMBA 'THE BOY WITH NO NAME'

D'WE K'LL HER!?

<We live in the mountains, and you are welcome there. If you choose to join us you may find "rest." It will not be an easy trip.>

AND

I SHON'T BE HERE.

F'MLY DEBT, JUS' PAY DEBTS... SO TIRED.

<The mountain is distant, cold and treacherous. These "Europeans" will not relent, but neither shall we.>

OHEMMAA NANNY

<We will protect you until you are well and able. Though in time you will have a choice of whether to live in your comfort zone or to destroy it.>

W-WHERE AM I 'NYWAY...?

IN

<You will live this war for the rest of your lives, but I leave this sliver of power in your hands, it will be your fight.

...AKWAABA... WELCOME TO XAYMACA!

TIME IS MASTER

GET 'CHA HEAD IN THE GAME

Robyn Smith is a Jamaican cartoonist, currently based in NYC. She has an MFA from the Center for Cartoon Studies and has worked on comics for the *Seven Days* newspaper, *College Humor*, and *The Nib*. She's best known for her mini-comic *The Saddest Angriest Black Girl in Town* and for illustrating Jamila Rowser's comic, *Wash Day*. Currently, she's working on more weird, sad autobiographical stuff and holding on to dreams of returning home, to the ocean.

ROBYN SMITH
Jamaica / United States

Instagram + Twitter   @RoBroSmo
robrosmo.tumblr.com

REFLECTIONS ON THE SEA

As I stare intensely into the blue, glistening sea, I see waves splashing all over the rocks. As I am leaving, I see the sun shining on the sea. The sea flows because of the wind. The sea is full of life, and it is truly beautiful. I will always love to see the glistening sea. You should now know that the sea is a wonderful thing, and you should see it too!

– Colette Walford, age ten

REFLECTIONS ON THE SEA

There is the sea,
and I am hungry.
It's time for bagels.

– Charles Walford, age thirteen

REFLECTIONS ON THE SEA

The tumultuous waves crash against
the moss-worn rocks of the shore as
I look out to sea.

The calming breeze of the morning does
not duet as sweetly with the troubled
tension of below as I had hoped.

Oh, to be still!

Blue-gray waters are not what I desire,

But alas, the crystal and comfort
of what we hope summer to be is
further and further,

A dream not come, and perhaps
never will come.

And yet, in the humidity of the day,
the sea weathers on.

And there is no doubt in my mind
that it continues, into the afternoon,
and midnight, and further 'til I'm gone.

Continues, continues, weathered
blue-gray.

– Kayla Walford, age fifteen

UNIDENTIFIED

WRITER / COVER ARTIST
JEROME WALFORD

ARTIST
ERIC BATTLE

COLORIST
BRYAN VALENZA

JEROME WALFORD
Writer / Cover Artist
Jamaica / United States

Unidentified is a short-short which condences our time and experiences into a single tale of desperation and hope. Thanks to Eric and Bryan for helping me to bring it to life.

ERIC BATTLE
Artist
United States

Eric Battle's career as an illustrator has covered the spectrum of comic books, and graphic novels, fashion illustration, children's books and advertising. His client list includes Legendary Motion Pictures & Comic Books, Marvel Comics, DC Entertainment, Top Cow, Valiant Entertainment, Dark Horse, and many more. Eric has illustrated many stories of popular icons, from Spider-Man and the X-Men, to Young Justice. His collaborators include World Fantasy Award-winning author Nnedi Okorafor and Game of Thrones author George R.R. Martin. Eric's project with Martin, *Wild Cards*, is being developed as a feature film by Universal/SyFy Films. Concurrently, Eric illustrated a ten-page comic book for Swarthmore College's Friends, *Peace & Sanctuary* art exhibition project.

BRYAN VALENZA
Colorist
Indonesia

Bryan Valenza has been a comic book colorist since 2012. In 2017 he founded the coloring studio BEYOND Colorlab, based in Jakarta, Indonesia. He currently occupies his time coloring various projects, including *Witchblade, Golgotha, Skies of Fire, InSEXts*, and *Mighty Morphin Power Rangers*.

rice

JEROME WALFORD
Writer / Artist
Jamaica / United States

Instagram + Twitter
@forwardcomix
forwardcomix.com

Jerome Walford graduated from Cornell University with a BFA (Bachelor of Fine Arts) degree with honors in 1996. Since then, he has worked steadily within advertising as a versatile consultant able to deliver digital art in nearly any style — illustrating marketing campaigns for Lenox Hill Hospital, Yahoo!, Nair, Discovery Channel, and other well-known brands.

In 2012, Jerome launched Forward Comix, an indie publisher, which quickly became known for stories with evocative worlds, relatable characters, and timely themes. Through Forward Comix Jerome launched his award-winning graphic novel series, *Nowhere Man*, which has garnered six Glyph nominations, a Glyph Comics Awards win for Best Male Character (2014), the Urban Comics Award, and two "Best of the Year" nominations on ComicAttack.net Some of his other works have been recognized by the Society of Illustrators, the Society of Illustrators of Los Angeles, and the *ImagineFX* magazine.

Jerome's most ambitious project, *Gwan Anthology*, has won many accolades, including a gold medal of excellence from the Independent Book Publisher Awards. The notable collection of art and stories, features immigrant and expat comic creators from around the world, sharing stories that shed light on aspects of the immigrant experience.

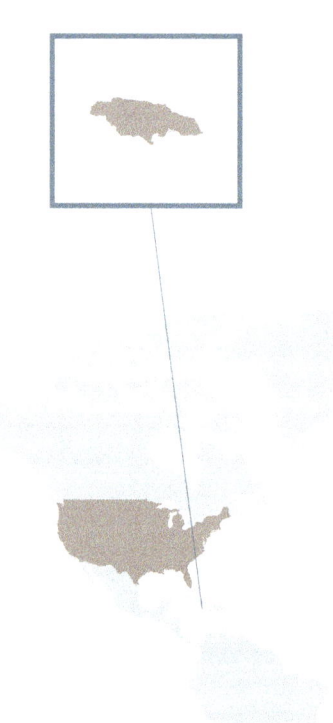

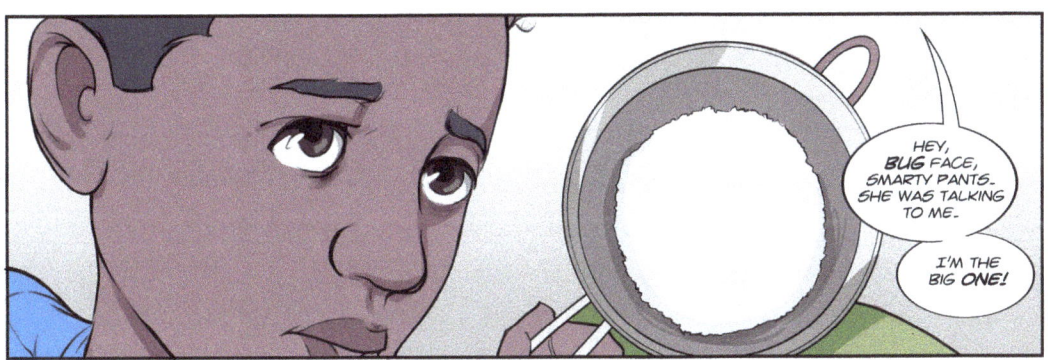

THE HOMS
Commissioned by Daniel Hom
Art by Jerome Walford

JUBILEE CHIU WONG
Commissioned by Stephanie Chiu Wong
Art by Jerome Walford

LYLE WALFORD AND GRANDCHILDREN
Commissioned by Lyle Walford
Art by Jerome Walford

Executive Producers

Stephanie Chiu Wong

Daniel Hom

Rebecca Perry Damsen

Jerome Walford

Lyle Walford

Producers

Lucius Haynes

Sylvia and Thomas Hom

Julie Jee

Mark Lim

Belinda Nieh

Jenevieve Que

Marilyn Richard Figueroa

Rich Walker Jr.

R.P. Wilson

David Wu

Managing Editor
Jerome Walford

Senior Editors
Rebekah Griffin Greene
Maya Rock

Assistant Editors
Lucius Haynes
Jenice Walford
R.P. Wilson

Special Thanks

Amy Walford

Nick Allen

R.P. Wilson & Lucius Haynes

Camilla Zhang & Kickstarter Team

Gwan Anthology Volume Two Entries

Sankoforration	John Jennings
The Little Children	Jerome Walford
Satori	Johny Tay, James O'Reilly
Ancestors	Miguel Guerra, Suzy Dias
Teef	Micheline Hess
Osun	Ayomide Omobo, Amari Harkness, Kokab Zohoori-Dossa
Mother Daughter	Jerome Walford
Organizing Is The New Cool	Craig Cflux Singleton
Scooter Down	Jerome Walford
Escaping Pandemonium	Abelard Alexis
Coming To Earth	Jarret Katz, Jerome Walford
Interwoven	Tara Naval, Paul Caggegi
His Heart Is Mine	Jerome Walford
The Play Boy	Li Zhang
The Witness	Anuj Shrestha
Tree Faces	Leonardo Gonzalez
Sunflowers	Kayla Walford
Monsterly	Damian Wampler, Elisabeth Mkheidze
Closet World	Matt Yocum, John Amor
Four Generations of Cawley	Julia Cawley
Little Swallow's Journey To Color	Yan Gabriella
Khanke, Iraq	100cameras
The Year of Reinvention	Ramon Gil
Hoodratz In Space	Erik Reeves
Seeds For A New Nubian Empire	Carles (CJ) Juzang
The Forge At Ile-Ife	Roye Okupe
Hostages Of The Sphere	Eric Wilkerson
Goddess Of Fertility	Hillary Wilson
Gladiis	Okera Damani
What's In A Name	Leah Yael Levy
Tomb Sweepers	Daniel Hom
Our Bodies Became Rice	Michael Watson
The Fox	Jasmine Haomin Shi
Graduation	Zheyu Wang
Potluck Bounty	Jerome Walford
Nanny	Mervyn McKoy
Get 'Cha Head In The Game	Robyn Smith
Reflections On The Sea	Charles Walford, Colette Walford, Kayla Walford
Unidentified	Jerome Walaford, Eric Battle, Bryan Valenza
Rice	Jerome Walford

CPSIA information can be obtained
at www.ICGtesting.com
Printed in the USA
LVHW071456230521
688268LV00014B/1704